Maude
and Walter

Maude
and Walter

by Zibby Oneal

illustrations by Maxie Chambliss

J.B. Lippincott　　　New York

For Walter and Maude—I mean Martha

Maude and Walter
Text copyright © 1985 by Zibby Oneal
Illustrations copyright © 1985 by Maxie Chambliss
Printed in the U.S.A. All rights reserved.
Designed by Trish Parcell
10 9 8 7 6 5 4 3 2 1
First Edition

Library of Congress Cataloging in Publication Data
Oneal, Zibby.
    Maude and Walter.

    Summary: Six stories chronicle some of the good
and some of the bad times Walter has with his little sister
Maude.
    1. Children's stories, American.   [1. Brothers and
sisters—Fiction]   I. Chambliss, Maxie, ill.   II. Title.
PZ7.0552Mau 1985   [E]   84-48357
ISBN 0-397-32150-3
ISBN 0-397-32151-1 (lib. bdg.)

Maude was small.
Walter was bigger.
Walter was Maude's big brother.

One day Walter was making a kite.
"I want to help," said Maude.
"No, Maude," said Walter, "go away."
"I want to make a kite, too," said Maude.
"No. You are too small. Go away, Maude."
Maude went away. Walter made his kite.

"My kite needs a tail," said Walter. "It needs a good long tail so it can fly. I will cut up a sheet. A sheet will make a good long tail."

Walter went to find his mother.

"I need a sheet," said Walter. "I want to cut up a sheet to make a tail for my kite."

"I don't have a sheet for you," said Walter's mother. "I don't have an old sheet to cut up."

"I have a sheet," said Maude.
Walter went to look at Maude's sheet.
"Here it is," said Maude. "It's a sheet of paper."

"No, no," said Walter. "That's not the right
kind of sheet. Go away, Maude."
Maude went away. Walter looked at his kite.

"My kite still needs a tail," said Walter. "My kite needs a tail so it can fly. I will find a necktie. A necktie makes a good tail."

Walter went to find his father.

"I need a tie," said Walter. "I need a tie to make a tail for my kite."

"I don't have a tie for you," said Walter's father. "I don't have an old tie."

"I have a tie!" said Maude.
Walter went to look at Maude's tie.
"Here it is," said Maude. "It's the tie in my shoe."
"No, no," said Walter. "That's not the right kind of tie. Go away, Maude."

Maude went away. Walter looked at his kite.

"My kite still needs a tail," said Walter. "My kite needs a tail so it can fly. It still does not have a tail."

"I have a tail!" said Maude.

"Maude, you do not have a sheet. You do not have a tie. You do not have a tail either, I bet. Where is your tail?"

"Here it is," said Maude. "It's my ponytail!"

"NO!" said Walter. "That is not the right kind of tail. GO AWAY!"

"My ponytail has a ribbon," said Maude. "A ribbon makes a good tail for a kite. Now I am going away."

8

"Wait!" said Walter. "Don't go away,
Maude. Give me your ribbon and you can fly
my kite."

"I have two ribbons," said Maude.

"You can fly my kite two times."

"They are long ribbons," said Maude.

"You can fly it two long times," said Walter.

"And I will not say 'Go away, Maude' again."

Walter built a tent.

He put up a sign that said "NO GIRLS."

"That's not fair," said Maude. "That is not fair, Walter."

Walter put a nail in his sign. He hammered the nail.

"You are breaking your promise again," Maude said.

"What promise?" said Walter.

He hammered the nail.

"I gave you my ribbons," said Maude.

"You flew my kite," said Walter.

"I went fishing with you," Maude said.

"I caught your fish for you," said Walter.

Maude sat on the swing and looked at Walter hammering the nail.

"You promised you would not say
'Go away, Maude' again."

"I didn't say it again," said Walter.

"When we were fishing you said 'Go away.'"

"I said 'Go home, Maude.' That's different."

"Now you have a sign that says 'NO GIRLS.'
You're putting it on your tent," said Maude.

"This is my club," Walter said. "My club is
not for girls."

"I am a girl," Maude said.

Walter hammered another nail. Maude
watched him.

"If there are no girls in your club, then I have to go away."

Walter hammered.

"If I have to go away, I will take my ribbons," Maude said. "I'll tie them on my ponytails."

Walter stopped hammering.

"I'll tie *all* my ribbons on my ponytails," said Maude.

Walter looked at his sign.

"My sign does not say 'Go away, Maude.'"

"It says 'No Girls,'" said Maude, "and I am a girl."

Walter looked at his kite. Walter looked at his sign.

"You are not a girl, Maude," said Walter. "You are a sister."

"Can I be in your club?" Maude said.

"Yes," said Walter.

"Then," said Maude, "I will not take my ribbons."

Walter made a new sign.
He put it on his tent.
The sign said

NO GIRLS EXCEPT SISTERS

III

Maude was sick. She had a cough.

"Too bad, Maude," Walter said. "Now you'll have to stay in bed all day."

"Now I'll miss a whole day at school, Walter."

Walter put on his coat to go to school.

Maude stayed in bed.

She coughed.

"Too bad, Maude," said Walter. "Now you'll have to take some cough medicine."

"The new cough medicine tastes like cherry soda," said Maude. "I like it."

Walter walked to school.

When school was over, Walter walked home.
Maude was still in bed.
She sneezed.

"Too bad, Maude," said Walter. "We had
chocolate milk for lunch at school."
"I had chocolate ice cream in bed at home,"
said Maude.
"And I have a new box of crayons.
And I have some new colored paper, too,"
she said.
"Oh," said Walter.

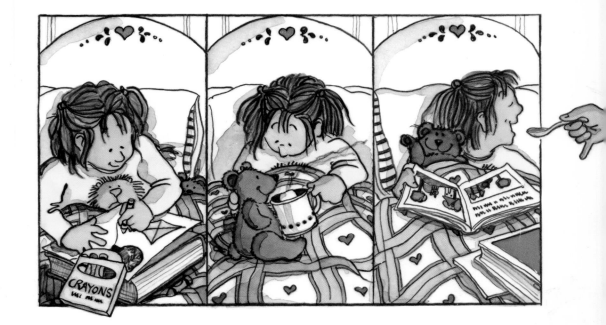

Maude drew a picture of a kite with her
new crayons.

She drew a picture of a tent.

She had a cup of hot chocolate with a
marshmallow on top.

She had a spoonful of cherry medicine.

Walter watched.

Then Walter coughed.

"Why are you coughing, Walter?" said
Maude.

"I think I am getting sick, too," said Walter.

"Too bad, Walter," said Maude. "Now you
will have to stay in bed and take medicine."

Walter looked at the crayons.

He looked at the hot chocolate with a
marshmallow on top.

He looked at the medicine as red as a
cherry.

Then Walter coughed again.

"Too bad, Walter," Maude said.

"Oh well," said Walter. "I don't really mind,
Maude."

IV

Maude had a new friend. His name was
Joe. Nobody could see him but Maude.

"Joe is not real. You made him up," said
Walter.

"Joe is one hundred feet tall," said Maude.

"Nobody is one hundred feet tall," said
Walter.

"Well," said Maude, "Joe is."

Maude saved Joe a seat in the car. She
saved him a seat at the table.

"Why do you need a friend named Joe?"
said Walter. "I am your friend."

"You are my brother."

"I am your brother *and* your friend."

"Joe is nice," said Maude.

"I am nice," said Walter.

"Joe never says 'Go away,'" said Maude.

Walter and Maude had beans for lunch.
Walter liked beans. Maude didn't.
   "Eat your beans, Maude," said Walter.
   "I can't eat them," said Maude.
   "Beans are good for you," said Walter.
   "I am saving my beans for Joe," said Maude.

Walter sat on the swing after lunch.
"Walter! Get up!" Maude screamed.
Walter got up. He looked at the swing.
"What's wrong?" said Walter.
"You are sitting on Joe! Joe is on the swing!
He wants me to swing with him," said Maude.

Joe went to the park. He went with Maude.
They borrowed Walter's kite.

"Where is my kite?" Walter said later.

"Joe borrowed it," said Maude.

"You know you should ask to borrow my kite."

"But Joe didn't know," Maude said.

Maude and Joe left books on the floor.
They left toys. They left apples.

"Now you must pick up," Maude's mother
said. "Walter will you help your sister?"

"Why doesn't Joe help Maude?" said
Walter.

"Joe is gone," said Maude. "Joe went to be
an astronaut. Will you help me pick up,
Walter?"

Walter helped Maude pick up the books.
He helped her pick up the toys and the
apples. Then Walter and Maude sat on the
swings.

"Is Joe coming back?" said Walter.

"No," said Maude. "He is not coming back.
You are my brother and you are my friend,
Walter, and I like you better."